D0952535

Dear Parents:

Congratulations! Your child is taking the first steps on an exciting journey. The destination? Independent reading!

STEP INTO READING® will help your child get there. The program offers five steps to reading success. Each step includes fun stories and colorful art or photographs. In addition to original fiction and books with favorite characters, there are Step into Reading Non-Fiction Readers, Phonics Readers and Boxed Sets, Sticker Readers, and Comic Readers—a complete literacy program with something to interest every child.

Learning to Read, Step by Step!

Ready to Read   Preschool–Kindergarten
• big type and easy words • rhyme and rhythm • picture clues
For children who know the alphabet and are eager to begin reading.

Reading with Help   Preschool–Grade 1
• basic vocabulary • short sentences • simple stories
For children who recognize familiar words and sound out new words with help.

Reading on Your Own   Grades 1–3
• engaging characters • easy-to-follow plots • popular topics
For children who are ready to read on their own.

Reading Paragraphs   Grades 2–3
• challenging vocabulary • short paragraphs • exciting stories
For newly independent readers who read simple sentences with confidence.

Ready for Chapters   Grades 2–4
• chapters • longer paragraphs • full-color art
For children who want to take the plunge into chapter books but still like colorful pictures.

STEP INTO READING® is designed to give every child a successful reading experience. The grade levels are only guides; children will progress through the steps at their own speed, developing confidence in their reading.

Remember, a lifetime love of reading starts with a single step!

Visit us on the Web!
StepIntoReading.com
rhcbooks.com

Educators and librarians, for a variety of teaching tools, visit us at RHTeachersLibrarians.com

ISBN 978-0-7364-4028-8 (trade) — ISBN 978-0-7364-8284-4 (lib. bdg.)
ISBN 978-0-7364-4029-5 (ebook)

Printed in the United States of America
10 9 8 7 6 5 4 3 2 1

DISNEY
FROZEN II

Spirits of Nature

by Natasha Bouchard

illustrated by the Disney Storybook Art Team

Random House 🏠 New York

There were once
four spirits of nature.
The spirits have not
been seen for many years.

Elsa's power is growing.

She blasts her magic.

It wakes the spirits!

The trolls tell Elsa
the spirits are upset.

Elsa must face the spirits.
She will go to the
Enchanted Forest.

Anna and Elsa
go north.
Their friends go, too.

They find the
Enchanted Forest
behind a wall of mist.

The four spirits are
wind, fire,
water, and earth.

The Wind Spirit
is playful and friendly.

The Fire Spirit

is small but mighty.

The Wind Spirit swirls
around the friends.
They fly into the air!

The Fire Spirit runs
through the forest.
Elsa chases its fire
with her ice power.

Earth Giants
are big and powerful.

The Water Spirit
is swift,
like a horse.

Earth Giants sleep
by the river.

Anna and Olaf float by.

They stay very quiet.

The Water Spirit swims
in the Dark Sea.
Elsa meets
the Water Spirit.

Elsa faced the spirits!
There will be peace
throughout the land.